HÄGAR THE HORRIBLE
HAPPY HOUR

BY
DIK BROWNE

JOVE BOOKS, NEW YORK

HÄGAR THE HORRIBLE: HAPPY HOUR

A Jove Book / published by arrangement with
King Features Syndicate, Inc.

PRINTING HISTORY
Tempo edition / January 1983
Charter edition / September 1984
Jove edition / October 1989

All rights reserved.
Copyright © 1973, 1976, 1977, 1981, 1982, 1983
by King Features Syndicate, Inc.
This book may not be reproduced in whole or in part,
by mimeograph or any other means, without permission.
For information address: The Berkley Publishing Group,
200 Madison Avenue, New York, New York 10016.

ISBN: 0-515-10225-3

Jove Books are published by The Berkley Publishing Group,
200 Madison Avenue, New York, New York 10016.
The name "JOVE" and the "J" logo
are trademarks belonging to Jove Publications, Inc.

PRINTED IN THE UNITED STATES OF AMERICA

10 9 8 7 6 5 4 3 2 1

NO USE CRYING OVER SPILLED MILK!
SNIFF
SNIFF

MILK?!
I'M TALKING BEER!
DIK BROWNE
2-19
© 1982 King Features Syndicate, Inc. World rights reserved.

I'M NOTHING BUT A SLAVE IN THIS HOUSE!
© 1982 King Features Syndicate, Inc. World rights reserved.
SO YOU KNOW WHAT YOU ARE!
I GIVE UP– WHAT'S LOWER THAN A SLAVE?
2-20
DIK BROWNE

HOW WAS YOUR DAY?
2-22
DIK BROWNE
© 1982 King Features Syndicate, Inc. World rights reserved.

STAY BEHIND THIS ROCK — THOSE ARCHERS ARE FAMOUS FOR THEIR ACCURACY!
© 1982 King Features Syndicate, Inc. World rights reserved.
CRACK!
ALSO THEIR STRENGTH
DIK BROWNE
2·23

DIK BROWNE
© 1982 King Features Syndicate, Inc. World rights reserved

2-24
WHAT ARE YOU LOOKING SO INNOCENT ABOUT ?!

I HAVE FACED TEN THOUSAND FOES! I HAVE TASTED BOTH VICTORY AND DEFEAT AND HAD MY FILL OF BOTH!

THAT'S GOOD BECAUSE YOU MISSED DINNER
2-25
DIK BROWNE
© 1982 King Features Syndicate, Inc. World rights reserved.

WHY SO HAPPY, HAGAR ?
I LIVED UP TO MY FAMILY MOTTO TODAY: "I GOT MINE!"
WHAT'S WRONG WITH YOUR PAL ?
OH... I GOT HIS, TOO!
DIK BROWNE
2-26

ARE YOU MAD ABOUT SOMETHING?
NO!
JUST ASKING...
DIK BROWNE
2-27
© 1982 King Features Syndicate, Inc. World rights reserved.

HAGAR, THE INSURANCE CLAIMS ADJUSTOR IS HERE

NOW, FIRST, WAS THERE ANY DAMAGE ?
2-1
DIK BROWNE

AS I LOOK BACK ON MY LIFE I REALIZE I'VE MISSED A LOT OF IMPORTANT THINGS
YEAH...
© 1982 King Features Syndicate, Inc. World rights reserved.

THAT'S BECAUSE A LOT OF PEOPLE ***HID*** THEIR IMPORTANT THINGS WHEN THEY SAW YOU COMING
2-2
DIK BROWNE

HEY! I'M HUNGRY! SERVE THE MEATBALLS!
SWACK!!
DIK BROWNE
NICE SERVE—
2-3
BOUNCE
PLOP

IT'S ME!
© 1982 King Features Syndicate, Inc. World rights reserved.
PLOP!
AW, C'MON! I'VE BEEN HOME ON TIME BEFORE!
2-4
DIK BROWNE

DIK BROWNE
2-5
GLUG
GLUG

SLURP!

I DO WISH YOU'D USE A COASTER!
DRIP
SPAT

HAMLET! DON'T TALK WITH YOUR MOUTH FULL... IT ISN'T CONSIDERED REFINED
BUT DADDY DOES IT

I REST MY CASE
2-6
WAF
HUR
WA!!
DIK BROWNE
© 1982 King Features Syndicate, Inc. World rights reserved.

I'M BACK FROM MY TRIP TO ICELAND, HELGA!
WHAT DID YOU BRING ME?

GUESS
DIK BROWNE
3-1

THESE STAINS IN THIS SHIRT SEEM TO BE GETTING EVEN WORSE!
HELGA, I LEFT SOME JELLY BEANS IN MY...
OH, YOU FOUND THEM!
3-2
DIK BROWNE

HAGAR! YOU'RE BACK! EVERYBODY MISSED YOU!

NOT EVERYBODY
DIK BROWNE
3-3

LET'S SEE...I'LL HAVE ORANGE JUICE, COFFEE, PANCAKES, MUFFINS...
BACON, EGGS, SAUSAGE, SALAD, COLD CUTS, BEER...
STILL EATING BREAKFAST?
I GOT UP TOO MUCH MOMENTUM AND SLID RIGHT ON INTO LUNCH!
3-4
DIK BROWNE

IS MY HAIR NEAT IN BACK ?
YEAH
IS MY HEM STRAIGHT ?
SURE SURE
~SIGH~ A HUSBAND IS NO SUBSTITUTE FOR A FLOOR-LENGTH MIRROR
3-5
DIK BROWNE
© 1982 King Features Syndicate, Inc. World rights reserved.

© 1982 King Features Syndicate, Inc. World rights reserved.
YOU KNOW— LIFE'S FUNNY!
YOU JUST HAVE A SICK SENSE OF HUMOR
DIK BROWNE
3-6

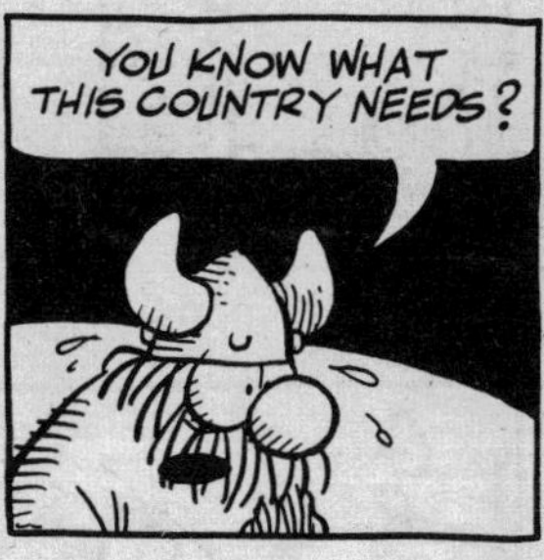
YOU KNOW WHAT THIS COUNTRY NEEDS?

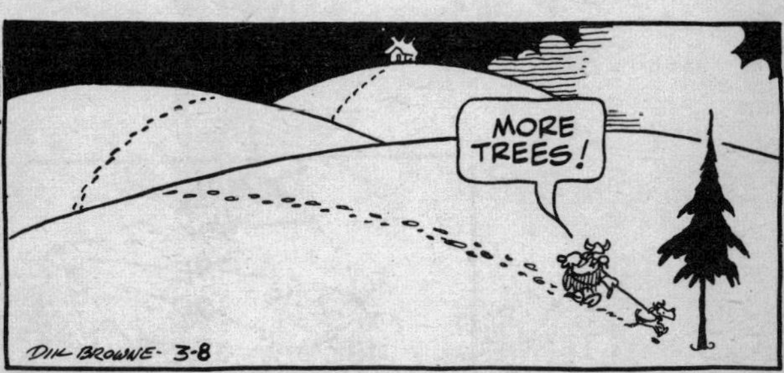
MORE TREES!
DIK BROWNE 3-8

POLLY WANTS A CRACKER
GRRRRR!
© 1982 King Features Syndicate, Inc. World rights reserved.
DIK BROWNE
SNERT WANTS ONE, TOO...
3-9

AH-CHOO!
WHAT IS IT WITH YOU, LUCKY EDDIE?

EVERY TIME WE INVADE ENGLAND YOU GET THE SNIFFLES!
3-10
DIK BROWNE
© 1982 King Features Syndicate, Inc. World rights reserved.

YOU CAN ALWAYS TELL WHEN YOUR FATHER IS AWAY ON A BUSINESS TRIP...

...THE PETS KNOW THERE WILL BE SOME LEFTOVERS
DIK BROWNE
3-11

YOU SAID, "TURN LEFT AT GREENLAND"
I GUESS I WAS WRONG

IT TAKES A FAT MAN TO ADMIT HE'S WRONG
THAT'S A *BIG* MAN, STUPID!!
3-12
DIK BROWNE

I HAVE TO GET MARRIED!

ALL MY FRIENDS ARE MARRIED AND IF I DON'T FIND A HUSBAND SOON I'LL JUST DIE!!
3-13
DIK BROWNE
© 1982 King Features Syndicate, Inc. World rights reserved.

THIS IS A 10-POUND SACK OF POTATOES—HEAVY, ISN'T IT?

THAT'S WHAT YOU CARRY AROUND ALL DAY—IN FAT! AND SIX MORE SACKS LIKE IT! THAT'S WHY YOU HAVE TO DIET!

AND STOP EATING THOSE POTATOES!
3-15
DIK BROWNE

HAGAR! GLAD YOU COULD MAKE THE PARTY! COME IN!

3-16
I GUESS YOU KNOW EVERYONE
DIK BROWNE

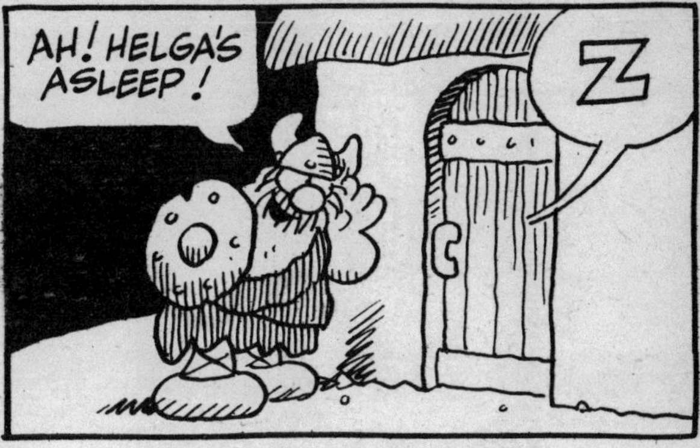
AH! HELGA'S ASLEEP!
Z

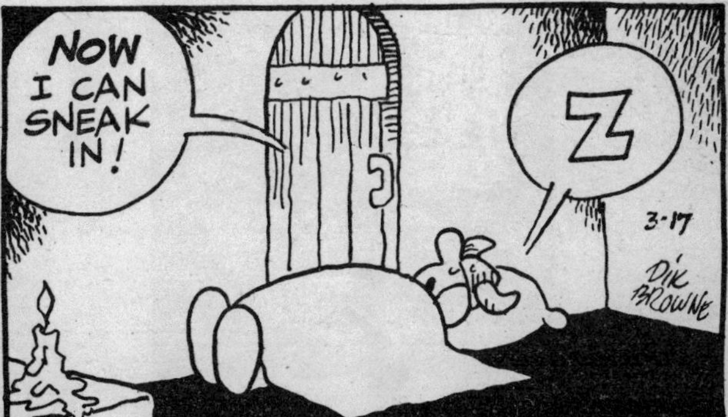
NOW I CAN SNEAK IN!
Z
3-17
DIK BROWNE

© 1982 King Features Syndicate, Inc. World rights reserved.
3-18
WHERE ARE WE, HAGAR ?
IF MY CALCULATIONS ARE CORRECT WE JUST ENTERED THE BLACK FOREST

STOP WORRYING! HALF THE THINGS PEOPLE FEAR NEVER EVEN HAPPEN
OH, REALLY?

WHAT ABOUT THE OTHER HALF?
3-19

THEY'LL KILL YOU!
DIK BROWNE

HOLD STILL!
OH, COME ON, HELGA!

IT'S HARD TO BE MACHO WITH NAME TAGS IN YOUR BEARSKIN!
DIK BROWNE
3-20

I'M HOME, HELGA! GUESS WHAT I BROUGHT YOU ?
A CAMEL-HAIR COAT ?!

NO...BUT YOU'RE CLOSE
3-22
DIK BROWNE

AH! THERE YOU ARE!

MITZI AND I WERE JUST PASSING BY
DIK BROWNE
3-23

HAGAR STILL HAS AN EYE FOR A PRETTY GIRL
YES

AHH....
3-24
DIK BROWNE

OK! POUR THE BOILING OIL!
WAIT! WAIT!

MY FRENCH FRIES!
3-25
DIK BROWNE

WHAT'RE YOU IN FOR ?
I'M A POLITICAL HUMORIST

OH... WHAT'S HE IN FOR ?
HE'S MY AGENT
3-26
DIK BROWNE

WHY ARE MEN SUCH ROTTEN HUSBANDS?
THEY SAY IT'S BECAUSE THEIR MOTHERS SPOIL THEM
I KNEW THEY'D FIND A WAY TO BLAME IT ON A WOMAN
DIK BROWNE
3-27

I DON'T UNDERSTAND WHY I PUT ON WEIGHT...
A LOT OF PEOPLE EAT MORE THAN I DO!
BUT IT TAKES A **LOT** OF PEOPLE TO DO IT
3-29
DIK BROWNE

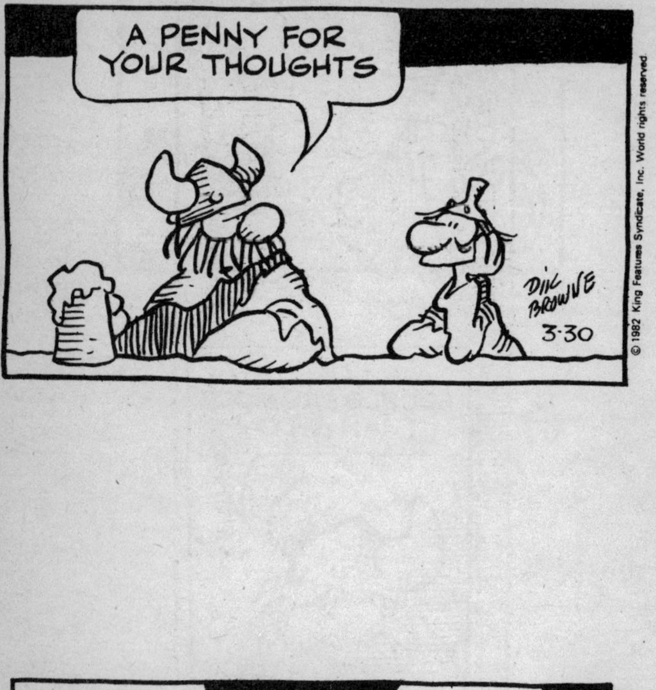
A PENNY FOR YOUR THOUGHTS
DIK BROWNE
3-30
FORGET IT!

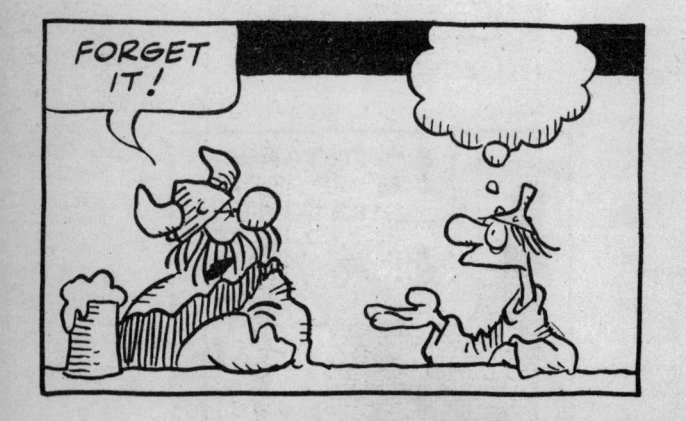

ON THIS SITE WILL BE ERECTED "STONEHENGE"
I HATE PROGRESS
3-31
DIK BROWNE
© 1982 King Features Syndicate, Inc. World rights reserved.

HI, HAGAR
HUH? DO I KNOW YOU, MISS?
IT'S ME— LADY GODIVA!
OH, I'M SORRY—I DIDN'T RECOGNIZE YOU
ARE YOU DOING SOMETHING DIFFERENT WITH YOUR HAIR?
DIK BROWNE
4-1

DIK BROWNE
© 1982 King Features Syndicate, Inc. World rights reserved.

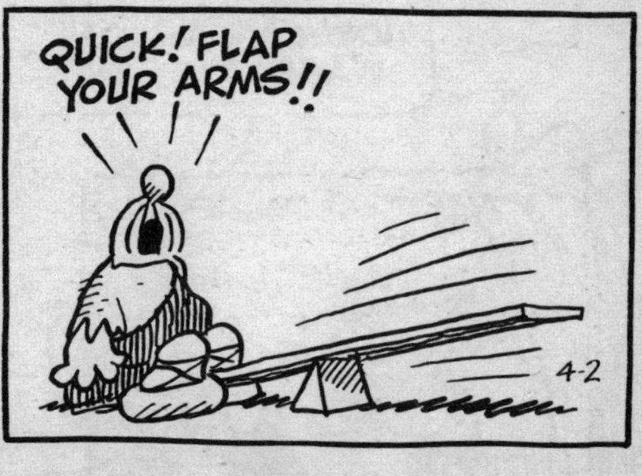
QUICK! FLAP YOUR ARMS!!
4-2

I WASHED IT—SATISFIED?
LET ME SEE THE OTHER HAND

HOW CAN ANYONE WASH ONE HAND?
DIK BROWNE
4-3
© 1982 King Features Syndicate, Inc. World rights reserved.

I'M GONNA MAKE YOU MY HOBBY!
DIK BROWNE 4-5
© 1982 King Features Syndicate, Inc. World rights reserved.

WAS IT FUN WHEN YOU WERE MY AGE?
FUN? ARE YOU KIDDING?!
© 1982 King Features Syndicate, Inc. World rights reserved.
IT WAS Fabulous
DIK BROWNE
I COULD EAT EVERYTHING!
4-6

HOW WOULD YOU LIKE YOUR STEAKS, GENTLEMEN?
DIK BROWNE 4-7

RAW OR VERY RAW?

DIK BROWNE 4-8
AH!
© 1982 King Features Syndicate, Inc. World rights reserved.

WHAT'S HIS PROBLEM, DR. ZOOK?
HE'S A WEREWOLF — POOR DEVIL!
GRRR.

CAN YOU DO ANYTHING FOR HIM?
SHAVE AND A HAIRCUT
DIK BROWNE 4-9
© 1982 King Features Syndicate, Inc. World rights reserved.

WE'RE IN TIME, LUCKY EDDIE!
BAR

WE JUST MADE THE "HAPPY HOUR"!
DIK BROWNE 4-10

THAT SMILE! THAT STRANGE, SECRET, ENIGMATIC SMILE THAT ONLY WOMEN HAVE.
WHY DO I FEEL HELPLESS, THREATENED? WHAT DOES IT MEAN?!!
YOUR MOTHER IS COMING–RIGHT?
4-12
DIK BROWNE

NOW, HERE'S THE PLAN... I'LL KNOCK ON THE DOOR AND WHEN THEY OPEN UP —
4-13

YOU BLOCK THE DOOR OPEN WITH YOUR FOOT

WHAT'CHA DOING, DAD ?
I WAS JUGGLING THESE ORANGES...
DIK BROWNE
© 1982 King Features Syndicate, Inc. World rights reserved.

AND I SEEM TO HAVE LOST ONE...
4-14

I LET HONI PRACTICE COOKING BREAKFAST —HOW ARE YOUR SCRAMBLED EGGS ?
DIFFERENT

I'VE NEVER HAD THEM WITH SHELLS SCRAMBLED, TOO.
4-15
DIK BROWNE

REPAIRS
I THINK WE LOCATED THE TROUBLE
DIK BROWNE
4-16
© 1982 King Features Syndicate, Inc. World rights reserved.

OH, STOP COMPLAINING, LUCKY EDDIE!

NOBODY ENJOYS TAKING INVENTORY
4-17
DIK BROWNE
© 1982 King Features Syndicate, Inc. World rights reserved.

...HALF A SNOWMAN... AND A FISH HOOK ... AND THE BACK OF A CAT...
GOOD... NOW, CAN YOU READ THE NEXT LINE ?
A
BJQ
HONXLI
ENYT4OT
4-19
© 1982 King Features Syndicate, Inc. World rights reserved.

DIK BROWNE
4-20
© 1982 King Features Syndicate, Inc. World rights reserved.
HAGAR! THAT MAN IS FLIRTING WITH ME!

WHAT'S THE WEATHER? SEE WHAT THE SKY LOOKS LIKE.
JUST ONE LITTLE CLOUD

WE BETTER WAIT HERE TILL IT BLOWS OVER
BAR
4-21
DIK BROWNE

WHATEVER HAPPENED TO THE THIN, HANDSOME, WITTY FELLOW I MARRIED YEARS AGO?

YOU MEAN THIS IS YOUR SECOND MARRIAGE, HELGA?
4-22
DIK BROWNE

WHAT'S DUTCH FOR FRIEND ?
VIJAND ?
VIJAND !
DIK BROWNE
THAT'S NOT IT !
4-23

HAMLET! DADDY HAS A LOT OF WORK TO DO!
DIK BROWNE

PUT YOUR PET SQUIRRELS BACK IN THEIR CAGE!
4-24
© 1982 King Features Syndicate, Inc. World rights reserved.

I'D LIKE TO HAVE HIM TRIMMED, CLIPPED, WASHED AND DE-FLEAED...

AND DO THE DOG, TOO...
DIK BROWNE
4-26
© 1982 King Features Syndicate, Inc. World rights reserved

REMEMBER, MEN— WE'RE IN ENEMY COUNTRY— WATCH OUT FOR TRICKS!
DIK BROWNE
4-27
© 1982 King Features Syndicate, Inc. World rights reserved.

ANOTHER DAY... ANOTHER DOLLAR...
SIGH
4-28
IT AIN'T WORTH IT...
© 1982 King Features Syndicate, Inc. World rights reserved.
DIK BROWNE

THAT WAS FUN—TOO BAD YOU MISSED YOUR DINNER
ARE YOU KIDDING?! I'M THE BOSS IN MY FAMILY AND MY DINNER IS ON THE TABLE NO MATTER WHEN I GET HOME!
DIK BROWNE
4-29

DID YOU COUNT NOSES ?
YES–IT STILL COMES OUT TO 23!

I'LL BET YOU COUNTED CARL TWICE
4-30
DIK BROWNE

DESSERT?
NO, NO! I'LL JUST HAVE COFFEE...
© 1982 King Features Syndicate, Inc. World rights reserved.

YOU KNOW... THE KIND WITH WHIPPED CREAM ON TOP... COOKIES ON THE SIDE... A CHERRY... MAYBE A SLICE OF...
YOU REALLY *ARE* STICKING ON YOUR DIET...
5-1
DIK BROWNE

IS SNERT A LAP DOG ?
HE USED TO BE...
DIK BROWNE

WHEN HAGAR HAD A LAP
5-3

MOTHER, THIS IS MY FRIEND "DIRTY DIRK"

DIK BROWNE 5-4
IS HE CONTAGIOUS?

WHAT'S IT ALL ABOUT? WHY AM I HERE?
YOU CAME IN FOR A FEW DRINKS ON THE WAY HOME —REMEMBER?
CHANGE THAT TO "WHY AM I HERE —WITH HIM?"
DIK BROWNE
5-5

I'M HOME, HELGA—ANYTHING EXCITING HAPPEN WHILE I WAS GONE ?
5-6
DIK BROWNE

THE TAX COLLECTOR WAS HERE
© 1982 King Features Syndicate, Inc. World rights reserved.

HURRY! HURRY! YOU'RE GONNA MISS IT!!
5-7
DIK BROWNE

THE TIDE IS GOING OUT FAST!

ISN'T THAT "HAGAR THE TERRIBLE"?
NO, NOT "TERRIBLE"— "HORRIBLE"! GET IT RIGHT!!
5-8
DIK BROWNE

YOU KNOW HOW TOUCHY PEOPLE ARE ABOUT THEIR NAMES

I'M HOME, HELGA
CAREFUL !! THE FLOOR'S WET !
© 1982 King Features Syndicate, Inc. World rights reserved.
DIK BROWNE
5-10
HOW WAS AFRICA ?

WHY DOES MAMA ALWAYS TELL ME TO CHEW WITH MY MOUTH CLOSED, DAD?
WOMEN HATE TO SEE ANYONE CHEW WITH THEIR MOUTH OPEN, SON
DIK BROWNE

THAT'S WHY MEN GROW HEAVY BEARDS AS SOON AS THEY CAN
5-11

I KNOW IT'S BEEN A LONG HARD TRIP, MEN
5-12

BUT CHEER UP—IT'S ALL DOWNHILL FROM HERE
DIK BROWNE

YOUR SHIELD AND SPEAR
NOT TODAY, DEAR— I'M TRAVELING LIGHT
5-13
DIK BROWNE

WHAT'S IN THE BAG?
LUNCH

WHAT'S THE TROUBLE? DOESN'T YOUR WIFE UNDERSTAND YOU?
WORSE...

DIK BROWNE 5-14
SHE DOES
© 1982 King Features Syndicate, Inc. World rights reserved.

CASTLES ARE O.K. — BUT THE WASH IS ALWAYS IN THE BEDROOM AND THE LAUNDRY IS IN THE MOAT
5-15
© 1982 King Features Syndicate, Inc. World rights reserved.
MY NEXT HOUSE IS GOING TO BE ALL ON ONE FLOOR
DIK BROWNE

... THAT'S BECAUSE GIRLS MATURE FASTER THAN BOYS.
DIK BROWNE
WHAT DOES THAT MEAN?
I DON'T KNOW... IT'S SOMETHING WOMEN SAY...

THEY AIN'T MAKING HOUSES LIKE THEY USED TO!
I'LL GO ALONG WITH THAT.
THEY'RE NOT MAKING ANYTHING LIKE THEY USED TO!
DIK BROWNE
OH, I WOULDN'T GO THAT FAR!

YOU **HAD** TO HAVE YOUR WIFE LAUNCH THE NEW BOAT, DIDN'T YOU? DIDN'T YOU?!
7-15 DIK BROWNE
© King Features Syndicate, Inc., 1977.

I DON'T UNDERSTAND MEN.
WHAT'S TO UNDERSTAND?
DIK BROWNE 12-13
JUST THINK OF THEM AS LITTLE BOYS
ROTTEN LITTLE BOYS!!

WHEN ARE YOU GOING TO GET MARRIED?
I'M WAITING FOR THE RIGHT MAN.
DIK BROWNE 11-14
SOMEDAY HE'LL COME ALONG—
AND THEN HE'S GOING TO PAY FOR MAKING ME WAIT!
©King Features Syndicate, Inc., 1973.

EVER THINK OF BUYING ONE OF THOSE?

ARE YOU KIDDING? HELGA WON'T EVEN LET ME HAVE A PUPPY DOG.
DIK BROWNE
9-3
©King Features Syndicate, Inc., 1973. World rights reserved.

TO GET A MAN THERE ARE THREE THINGS A GIRL NEEDS.
DIK BROWNE

THE FIRST IS GOOD LOOKS.

AND IF YOU GOT THAT THE OTHER TWO DON'T MATTER.

HAGAR
HERE'S THE TARGET NOW!
I'M SORRY WE'RE LATE
4-4 DIK BROWNE
WHICH WAY DID YOU COME?
BY WAY OF SHERWOOD FOREST
© King Features Syndicate, Inc., 1977. World rights reserved.

GO! I WOULDN'T ASK YOU TO DO ANYTHING I WOULDN'T DO MYSELF!
© King Features Syndicate, Inc., 1977.
AFTER ALL, YOU'RE LIKE A PART OF ME!
AW... THAT'S NICE
POW!
POP!
DIK BROWNE 4-8
WHAT PART?

THOSE ARE THE *HAVES* AND WE ARE THE *HAVE-NOTS!!*

WHO ARE *THOSE* GUYS?
© King Features Syndicate, Inc., 1977. World rights reserved.

DIK BROWNE 4·9
OH, THOSE ARE THE *HAVE-LESS*

HAGAR
WE DON'T WANT TO FIGHT... YOU DON'T WANT TO FIGHT... WHY DON'T WE JUST SHAKE HANDS?
© King Features Syndicate, Inc., 1977.

DIK BROWNE
1-10
WATCH IT! IT'S A TRICK

HAGAR
LUCKY EDDIE, WHAT ARE YOU DOING?
TEACHING SNERT A TRICK
DON'T YOU KNOW YOU CAN'T TEACH AN OLD DOG NEW TRICKS?
© King Features Syndicate, Inc., 1976.
DIK BROWNE 12-20
MAYBE IF I STARTED WITH SOMETHING SIMPLER...